KT-224-694

A FORD & KEANE MYSTERY

THE BLACK PHONE

7000398O371X

First published 2012 by A & C Black,
an imprint of Bloomsbury Publishing plc
50 Bedford Square
London WC1B 3DP

www.bloomsbury.com

Copyright © 2012 A&C Black
Text copyright © 2012 James Lovegrove
Illustrations copyright © 2012 Sean Longcroft

The right of James Lovegrove and Sean Longcroft to be identified
as the author and illustrator of this work has been asserted by them
in accordance with the Copyrights, Designs and Patents Act 1988.

ISBN 978-1-4081-6333-7

A CIP catalogue for this book is available from the British Library.

All rights reserved. No part of this publication may be
reproduced in any form or by any means – graphic, electronic
or mechanical, including photocopying, recording, taping or
information storage and retrieval systems – without the prior
permission in writing of the publishers.

This book is produced using paper that is made from wood
grown in managed, sustainable forests. It is natural, renewable and
recyclable.The logging and manufacturing processes conform
to the environmental regulations of the country of origin.

Printed by CPI Group (UK), Croydon, CR0 4YY

1 3 5 7 9 10 8 6 4 2

A FORD & KEANE MYSTERY

THE BLACK PHONE

JAMES LOVEGROVE

A & C BLACK • LONDON

CHAPTER 1

THE CRYING GIRL

Frankie was pushing Seb home from school when they came across the crying girl.

She was sitting on the kerb, just round the corner from Seb's house. Her head was in her hands. Her long blonde hair shook as sobs shuddered through her body.

Frankie halted and Seb applied the brake on his wheelchair.

The girl was Tara Adamski, a Year 7 student like they were. She was American, and she had been at Seb and Frankie's school since September.

Tara was the most beautiful girl Seb had ever seen. She was tall and tanned, and had spectacular teeth, as white and even as chewing gum pieces. Her accent was thick and slow and sweet, like golden syrup.

He'd been a little bit in love with her from the day she arrived. He wasn't sure she even knew he existed. But he was happy to admire her from a distance. Now here she was, crying her eyes out in the street.

"Tara?" he said.

She looked up. Even though her face was puffy and streaked with tears, it was still lovely enough to take Seb's breath away.

"What's the matter?"

"Oh Seb," Tara sniffed. "Darn it, I wish you hadn't seen me like this. It's nothing. Just... dumb stuff."

"Doesn't look like 'nothing' to me," Frankie said. "What's going on?"

"You homesick?" Seb asked.

"No, it ain't that," Tara said. "I mean, sure, I miss all my friends back home. But we keep in touch. It's not so bad."

"So, why are you crying?"

"You can tell us," Frankie added. "We're good listeners."

"I know." Tara wiped her eyes with the back of one hand. "I know about you guys. Ford and

6

Keane. You're, like, detectives, right? You solve mysteries, right wrongs, do good."

Seb felt a burning glow of pride. Tara Adamski had heard of him! She knew what he did!

"That's us," he said. "If you've got a problem, Ford and Keane can help. Missing jewellery, lost pet, stolen wallet, strange goings-on next door – you name it, we solve it. Once Frankie and I are on the case, we won't stop until we've *owww!*"

Frankie had just rapped him sharply on the head with her knuckles.

"Why did you do that?" Seb complained.

"Tara doesn't want to hear you blah-blah-blah-ing on about what we do. She wants to talk. Don't you, Tara?"

"Yeah," Tara said. "Yeah, I do. That's why I was waiting here, as a matter of fact. I was hoping you two would come along. 'Specially you, Seb. Everyone says you're smart, a regular Einstein."

Seb preened.

"And I could really do with some help," Tara went on, looking imploringly at Seb. "It sounds crazy, but somebody's after me. They've got it in for me. I think they might even want me dead!"

CHAPTER 2

TEXT CRIME

In the Annex at the back of Seb's house, Seb and Frankie listened while Tara explained.

"It started a week ago," Tara said. "I got this text, see, on my cell. My mobile, as you Brits say. Unknown caller. The text said…"

She started trembling.

"It's OK," Seb soothed. "Take your time."

"Why don't I just show you instead?"

Tara fished her mobile from her pocket. It was a top-of-the-range smartphone. Its jet black shell was smattered with clear-coloured crystals, like stars in the night sky. She scrolled through her inbox and selected a message.

Seb read the text, with Frankie peering over his shoulder.

```
u r a stuk up yank cow. every1
hates u. y don't u just die?
```

"Nice," said Frankie.

"That was only the first," said Tara. "It's way from being the worst."

"How long have they been coming?" Seb asked.

"The past ten days or so."

"And how many have there been in all?"

"About twenty so far, I guess."

"Can I look at them?"

"Sure. Any text that isn't listed under someone's name, just a number, that's one."

Seb inspected the messages. The sender hated Tara with a passion. He – or she – called her awful names, described her as stupid and ugly, and made ominous-sounding threats.

One of the texts said Tara should go back to America and stop stinking up Britain. Another wished that she would have a terrible car accident and be scarred for life. Yet another talked about how it would be great if she could do everyone a favour and just kill herself.

Seb was shocked. How could anybody write such things? And what's more, about a girl as dazzling as Tara Adamski?

"You've gone to the police, of course," he said.

"My mom and pop insisted," Tara said, nodding. "Waste of time. The cops said, not their problem. A school matter."

"So you took it to Mrs Broomfield?" Frankie said. Mrs Broomfield was the headmistress.

"Uh-huh," said Tara. "That was a big fat bust too. It's obvious it's somebody at school sending the messages, but she was all like, 'What am I going to do, punish *everybody*?' She told me to try the cops."

"Police say it's the school's problem, school says it's the police's." Seb sighed hard. "Typical."

"Did you try calling back on the number?" Frankie asked.

"Uh-huh," said Tara, nodding. "Nobody picked up."

"They're probably just using that phone to do the bullying," said Seb. "Bought it specially for that purpose."

"So that's why I've come to see you guys," Tara said. "I reckon you're my last hope."

"What do you want us to do?" Frankie said.

"Find this creep," Tara said forcefully. "Find him and get him to stop. I don't think I can stand it much longer. I can't sleep. I'm scared to check my phone. I feel like everyone at school's staring at me, *glaring* at me. I... I'm even beginning to think maybe I *would* be better off dead. You know, if folks hate me that much..."

She started to cry again. Seb wheeled himself over to a shelf and grabbed down a box of tissues. Everything in his Annex was the right height for a 12-year-old in a wheelchair. The whole room had been built with Seb's disability in mind, from the extra-wide doorway to the specially designed computer desk.

He handed Tara the box of tissues. She took it gratefully and blew her nose.

Even her nose-blowing, Seb thought, was attractive.

"Don't say things like that," he told her. "This rat-bag wants you to feel worthless. He's getting his kicks making you doubt yourself. The only way he'll win is if he sees you give in."

"Seb's right," said Frankie. "We know what we're talking about. We've both of us been there."

"You have?" said Tara.

"Oh yeah. I've been given stick 'cause I'm big and mixed race and don't have a dad. Seb, 'cause he's in a wheelchair. There are bullies out there who'll pick on you for whatever reason – you look different, you speak different – anything. Don't let them grind you down."

"This person's scaring you," said Seb, "he's making you miserable, but he can't *really* hurt you. All he's got is words."

"But what if it isn't just words?" said Tara. "What if he gets bored of texting and tries to make it, you know, physical?"

"That'd be something else. But we're not there yet, and Frankie and I are going to make sure it doesn't go that far. Now, I suppose you tried blocking the caller number, yes?"

Tara nodded. "But he just started using another phone. See? There's one number for the first three days. Then I blocked it. Next day the texts started coming in again, from a different number. And I reckon if I block that second number he'll start using a third, and so on. It'll never end."

"How about changing your own number?" Frankie suggested.

"You think I haven't thought of that?" the American girl retorted. "But seeing as he got hold of this number, I doubt he'd have trouble getting hold of another."

"Also, you shouldn't have to do that," Seb said. "Why should you have to be mucked around

13

because of some idiot? Some idiot who can't even spell."

There were words spelled incorrectly in almost all of the texts. One or two might just have been mistakes. Most, however, seemed evidence of poor literacy skills.

"Yeah," said Tara. She braved a smile. "I knew you'd understand, Seb. I knew you'd care."

"You bet I care," Seb replied. "We're going to nail this sucker, Tara, I promise you that. You may have struck out with the police and Mrs Broomfield, but it won't be 'third strike and you're out' with Seb Ford and Frankie Keane, no sir!"

* * *

"'Nail this sucker'?" Frankie echoed, after Tara had left. "'Third strike and you're out'? 'No sir'? What are you *like*, Seb?"

Seb shrugged, slightly embarrassed. "Sorry. Don't know what came over me. Suddenly I went all American."

Frankie gave a sly smile. "You weren't by any chance trying to suck up to Tara? Impress her maybe? Just a little?"

Seb's cheeks flared red. "No idea what you mean."

"Oh come off it!" Frankie snorted. "Anyone can see you like her. And who can blame you? She's a stunner. Hollywood-grade looks."

"She does want to be in movies when she's older," Seb admitted.

"Trust you to know that."

"Everyone knows it. And she can act, too. She's got the lead in this year's musical, hasn't she? So she must be good."

"Either that or she did her twinkly-eye, flashy-teeth thing on Mr O'Hare at the casting auditions, and he fell for it too."

"Eurgh!" Seb pulled a face. "That's nasty. Slaphead O'Hare's, like, thirty-five. *Ancient.* Anyway, what do you mean by 'too'? Are you saying she was flirting with me just now?"

Frankie fixed him with a look: *well, duh!*

"She was not," Seb said, then added, "Was she?"

Frankie rolled her eyes. "Come on, lover boy," she said. "Head in the game. We've got work to do!"

15

CHAPTER 3

THREE TEXTS

Tara had left the black, crystal-encrusted phone with them. Seb had promised he would return it to her the next morning, outside the school gate. He was pleased about this. It gave him an excuse to see her again soon. Also, everyone would see him talking to her, which would earn him some cool points.

Frankie watched as Seb synched the phone with his PC via a USB cable. He pulled up a list on the monitor – a log of all the calls and texts that had been made and received on the phone.

He selected the incoming texts that originated from the two numbers Tara had flagged, opened them and printed off the contents.

"You're not going to look at any of the other texts?" Frankie said. "Mightn't there be clues there?"

"It's Tara's private stuff. We're detectives, not nosey parkers."

Seb began poring over the messages. Frankie went to the kitchen, made herself a drink and a sandwich, had a nice chat with Seb's mum, and came back to the Annex half an hour later to find Seb still poring over them. Seb's powers of concentration were amazing. Frankie was more at the ADHD end of things.

"Right," Seb said. "I've singled out three of these. Take a look."

The first said:

```
u think ur so pritty but you
aint. u only got nice teeth like
that coz Daddy payed 4 em
```

The second said:

```
u dont diserve 2 b sandy. ur the
1 that we dont want ha ha ha
```

The third said:

```
u shouldent of acused L of
copeying off u in chemistry.
```

```
go sit sumwhere else in the
labouratory, or else
```

"God, it makes my blood boil," Frankie said through clenched teeth. "If there's one thing I hate – really hate – it's bullies."

Seb knew this from personal experience. On his very first day at Charrington Secondary, a group of boys had started to pick on him. He was trying to get his wheelchair up the school's access ramp, but it had snowed recently and the ramp was coated with ice. He kept slipping backwards.

The boys jeered at him and called him "steel wheels" and then other, nastier names. Seb did his best to ignore them. First day at a new school. He didn't want to make waves.

Then the boys grabbed the wheelchair. Seb was helpless. He wished he hadn't told his mum to drop him at the gate and drive off. He wished he'd listened to her when she offered to push him all the way into school.

The boys shoved the wheelchair to the foot of the ramp. Then they started jerking it up and down and spinning it round in circles. There were no teachers in sight. Other kids just strolled by, looking the other way. They didn't want to get involved.

Then, out of nowhere, Frankie appeared. Without a word, she strode up to the bullies and punched the largest of them in the nose. Blood poured out and the boy fell to the ground, shrieking. The rest of the boys scurried away in alarm.

"They won't be bothering you again," Frankie told Seb. "And if they do, let me know and I'll sort them out."

Seb wasn't sure what to make of this sturdy girl with tightly curled hair. "Thanks," he said, "but I was handling it."

"No you weren't, you were pretending it wasn't happening. That's not the same as handling it."

"Won't you get into trouble?" Seb said. "That kid will tell a teacher who hit him."

Frankie shrugged. "No, he won't. And even if he did, I'll tell Mrs Broomfield why I did it, and she'll believe me, not him. That was Greg Stubbs. He's got a reputation."

"I suppose I'd know that if I wasn't a newbie," said Seb.

"Yeah well, serves you right for starting so late."

"Hey, not my fault. My dad's company just relocated him, smack in the middle of the school year. Sebastian Ford, by the way." Seb stuck out his hand. "Although I prefer Seb."

Frankie shook it. "Francesca Keane, but call me Frankie, because if you don't I'll hit you and all."

"Oh, um, OK." Seb winced. "You have a very strong grip, Frankie."

Frankie beamed. "I punch hard too." The bell rang for classes. "Want me to give you a push?" She saw the look on his face. "Or possibly you don't need any help."

"I can manage," said Seb. He eyed the ramp. Like a ski slope, it seemed. All slick, white and slippery. And he was still rattled after his encounter with Greg Stubbs and pals. "Then again..."

Seb and Frankie had been firm friends ever since. When Seb decided his calling in life was to be an amateur detective, there was only one person he wanted as his partner.

* * *

"So?" he said now, after he'd given Frankie time to study the three texts.

"Well, the first one, about Tara's teeth? That says jealous to me."

"Me too," said Seb. "Lots of American kids have their teeth fixed like that. You know, made all straight and white. Over there they crack jokes about how bad British people's teeth are."

"My teeth aren't bad," Frankie pointed out.

"Yeah, they're lovely, but by American standards they're still just average."

Frankie pouted.

"What about text number two?" Seb said.

"Well, it's obvious, isn't it?" said Frankie. "This year's musical is *Grease*, and Tara bagged the female lead, Sandy. You, of course, will be right there in the front row for every performance, clapping till your hands fall off."

Seb's cheeks flushed pink. "I don't know what you're talking about."

"'Cause she's your girlfriend," Frankie mocked.

"She is not."

"She is and you *lurve* her."

"Let's focus," Seb said. "'You're the one that we don't want.' That's a reference to the song in *Grease* – 'You're The One That I Want'. So

22

whoever this cyber-bully is, he's familiar with the musical. And when I say 'he', I also mean 'she'."

"You think it could be a girl?"

"Why not? Girls can be worse bullies than boys. Boy bullies usually just duff you up. Girl bullies use mind games, and that can do more harm than a thump."

Frankie nodded, knowing only too well what Seb was saying. Girls' tongues were sharp. They knew what stung.

"And finally," Seb said, "text three. Anything strike you about that one?"

"The really bad spelling."

"Yes, the spelling *is* interesting. But that's not all."

"Tara caught someone cheating off her in an exam and made a big fuss about it."

"Exactly," said Seb. "And...?"

"If we can find out who this 'L' is, then we've got a likely suspect – someone with a grudge against Tara."

"But the text doesn't say 'me', it says 'L'. Implying it was someone else – anyone who knew about her accusing this 'L' of cheating."

"Yes, but they're trying to hide their identity,

aren't they? If he – or she – had said 'me', that'd be a confession right there."

"Yes," said Seb. "That was my thinking too."

"Have I done well, Master Yoda?"

"*Very* well you have done, young Jedi."

They laughed.

"Although..." Seb's face creased in a frown. "Isn't a bit curious that Tara didn't draw our attention to that text? It seems to point almost directly to the sender."

"Maybe she was just too upset."

"Yes. This bullying is messing with her head and she's not thinking logically."

"But we are," Frankie stated.

Seb nodded in agreement. "I'll ask Tara about it tomorrow."

CHAPTER 4

NO PRESSURE

He did ask Tara about "L" the next day, when he returned her phone to her at the school gate.

"Oh, yeah," Tara said. She looked downcast. "Yeah, guess I ought to have said something. Sorry."

"It's OK," said Seb. "Who is 'L'?"

"Luke Waterlow. Couple of weeks back, Mr Fairley set us a surprise chemistry test. Halfway through, I noticed Luke out of the corner of my eye. He sits next to me. He was taking a sneaky peek at my paper then scribbling down the answer. First time, I thought I was maybe imagining it. But then five minutes later I caught him doing it again. So I stuck up my hand and told Mr Fairley."

"What did Mr Fairley do?"

"Separate us," said Tara. "And made both of us stay behind after class so's we could, he said, 'discuss the matter'. Which we did, except Luke accused *me* of cheating off of *him*. Me! Like I need to cheat in chem. My pop's a real chemist, you know that? He invents synthetic fabrics for the clothing industry. Chemistry's in my blood, you could say. The idea of me cheating in a chem exam. Ridiculous!"

Seb found himself nodding in agreement, even though he had no idea how good Tara was at chemistry, or any other subject.

"Do you..." Tara dropped her voice, as if afraid she might be overheard. "Do you think it's Luke who's doing this to me? To get his own back?"

"Maybe," Seb replied, "and he used the 'L' in his text to throw you off the scent."

"Gosh."

There was something incredibly appealing about the way Tara said that word – *gosh*. No one but an American could have put so much feeling into it, Seb thought, or made it sound so goofy and yet so serious.

"Now why didn't *I* think of that?" Tara went on. She was deeply impressed. "Let me tell you,

you are one smart cookie, Mr Seb Ford. Is it OK – would you mind – if I gave you a hug?"

Seb couldn't think of a single reason why not. Tara stooped and embraced him. She smelled terrific. The perfume she was wearing was flowery and exotic. Her long blonde hair fell softly, thrillingly, against his neck. Other kids made smooching sounds and "woooo" noises as they filed past. Seb didn't care. He was loving this. It was just how he'd imagined today's meeting with Tara would work out. No, *better* than he'd imagined. Way better.

Tears glistened in Tara's big blue eyes as she straightened up. "If it *is* Luke and you can stop him doing this," she said, "then I'll be in your debt forever, Seb."

"Th-that's the general plan," Seb stammered. "Stopping him, I mean. Not the debt part. Though that'd be nice. Not that I want you owing me anything, Tara," he added hurriedly. "But just knowing that I'd helped, and you were, you know, grateful. No, not grateful. Relieved. I should stop talking now, shouldn't I?"

"You're cute," said Tara. "One thing, though. I've got to tell you, my poppa, he's not happy about any of this. He said he's going to be talking

to his lawyer today about bringing a private prosecution against whoever's doing this."

"Can he do that?"

"Sure he can," said Tara. "Why not? Money's no object. And if we can't figure out who the culprit is, then he'll sue the school. Because the school's done nothing about the bullying. It's been 'remiss in its duties'."

"Blimey," said Seb. "You think he'll really go through with it?"

"'Course he will. My poppa always gets what he wants. I just thought you should know."

"Yeah." Seb whistled through his teeth. "So, no pressure then."

"Hey, I wouldn't have mentioned it if I didn't think you could handle it."

Tara patted Seb's head, gave his nose a gentle tweak, and walked away. Her hair tumbled down her back, shimmering with every step she took, like a long blonde waterfall.

Seb watched her go. Then, heaving a sigh, he trundled his wheelchair through the gate.

CHAPTER 5

SUSPECT ONE: CHEAT

Seb and Frankie met up at mid-morning break. Seb brought her up to speed on his conversation with Tara. Then they went in search of Luke Waterlow.

Luke was out in the playground, kicking a ball about with some mates.

"Quick word?" Frankie asked.

Luke sidled over. "What do you want?" He was a big lad, very sporty. His hair was coils of copper wire, and there were so many freckles on his face that hardly any pale-coloured skin showed at all.

"Just a couple of questions," said Seb, "if you don't mind."

"About?"

"Tara Adamski."

Luke scowled. "I've got nothing to say about that girl." He turned to rejoin the football game.

"Wait," said Frankie. She grabbed Luke's arm.

Luke gave her a look that could have soured milk. "Better let go, Keane. I don't normally hit girls, but..."

Luke was a tough customer. He sometimes mingled with Greg Stubbs's crowd.

"Just listen, Luke, please," Seb said. "We'd like to know about the chemistry test, that's all. We'd like to hear your side of the story."

"My side?" said Luke with a sneer. He wrenched his arm out of Frankie's grasp. "My side is that Tara told Homer Fairley I was looking at her paper." Mr Fairley's nickname was Homer because he looked a lot like Homer Simpson, unfortunately for him.

Seb chose his words carefully. "Which you weren't."

"Does it make any difference?" Luke spat. "Fairley believed her. He looked at our tests side by side. He said we'd got several of the same questions right, and several wrong the same way. He reckoned one of us must have been cheating, and who do you think ended up on report?"

"You," said Seb.

"Of course me. He'd never have suspected Golden Girl, would he?"

"But didn't you claim *she* was cheating?" said Frankie.

"Well, I had to say *something*, didn't I? Maybe she was. I thought she was sneaking me sideways looks during the test. What's it to you anyway? You two doing your usual thing? Sticking your noses into other people's business?"

"We're in the process of an investigation," Seb admitted.

Luke jabbed a finger at him. "Well, leave me out of it, Sherlock. You too, Miss Marple."

He strode off, but after three paces he stopped and swung round.

"I'm not a cheat," he said. "And I'll tell you this for free. I don't like that girl much, but I know someone who hates her even more."

"Who?" said Frankie.

"Greg. Greg Stubbs. Way he goes on about her, it's like she's his mortal enemy or something."

* * *

"Greg Stubbs?" said Frankie as she and Seb headed back across the playground. "Really? I

32

didn't know he and Tara had any contact. They don't have anything in common apart from they're both Year Seven."

"Could be Luke's pointing the finger at someone else so we don't think it's him. That's what guilty criminals often do."

"You reckon Luke's guilty?"

"Well, he fits the profile," Seb said. "He has an aggro streak. He has a motive. Also, he's not that bright, is he?"

"Meaning?"

"It would explain the bad spelling in the texts. But also, why would Tara try and copy his test answers? She'd be mad to."

"So that stuff about her sneaking looks at his work..."

"Luke said it himself. 'I had to defend myself.' He was in a tight spot, so he made up a lie. Fairley saw through it, naturally. Homer may be a walking advert for WeightWatchers, but he's no fool."

"But what if Luke's right about Greg?" said Frankie.

"That's what we've got to find out."

Frankie grimaced. "We're going to speak to Greg, aren't we? That's next on our to-do list."

34

"'Fraid so."

"Do we have to?"

"It's a lead," said Seb, "and a good detective always follows up a lead."

"I know, but... Greg Stubbs."

"You scared, Frankie?"

"No. You?"

"Of course not."

Each of them knew the other was fibbing.

CHAPTER 6

SUSPECT TWO: HARD MAN

Greg Stubbs was an easy person to find. If he wasn't in lessons, the dining hall or detention, he was hanging out with his cronies on the far side of the playing field, near the fence. During free time, Stubbs's gang liked to put as much distance as possible between them and the school buildings.

So that was where Seb and Frankie went, straight after lunch.

As they approached the spot, they looked in vain for Greg. Other members of his gang were there, lounging about on the grass, all insolent and menacing. They fixed Seb and Frankie with hard stares. There was no sign of Greg, though.

Then he appeared, emerging from a clump of shrubbery next to the fence.

"What're you two after?" Greg demanded. Even from several metres away, he reeked of cigarette smoke. "Who gave you permission to be here?"

"Yeah," said one of his mates, Skelly Cracknell. "Didn't you know? This is a no wheels zone."

The whole gang chortled.

Seb tried to let the insult slide over him. Out of the corner of his eye he saw Frankie stiffen. Knowing her, one more wisecrack like that and she would start a fight. A fight which she had no hope of winning.

"Listen," Seb said, "we don't want any trouble."

"Shouldn't have come here then, should you?" said another of the gang members, Benny Gorman – also known as Benny Bigmouth. Benny's tie was knotted so tightly and crookedly, it looked as though he'd tried to strangle himself.

"We just need some information," Seb said. His heart was beating fast. This could easily go wrong.

He remembered how Greg and company had attacked him on his very first day at Charrington

Secondary. He was sorely tempted to grab the hand rims on his wheelchair and push himself out of there as fast as he could.

"Yeah," Frankie said. "We just want to ask you something and then we'll be out of your hair."

"My hair? That supposed to be funny?" Greg had an overall number 4 buzz cut. It made his scalp look like a fuzzy beach ball. "That some kind of saddo joke?"

He strode up to Frankie, puffing out his chest. They stood eye to eye.

"I still owe you from last year," he said. "That sneaky sucker punch you gave me when I wasn't looking." He clenched his fists. "Now'd be a good time for a little payback."

Frankie stood her ground. She'd punched Greg that time because she'd been too outraged to worry about the consequences. She was scared now. All the same, she refused to back down. Frankie Keane was no coward.

"Tell us about Tara Adamski," she said. She was amazed at how calm her voice sounded. "Word is, you and she don't get on."

"Tara?" Greg blinked. "Who told you that?"

"It's going around," Frankie said. "Tara's done something to annoy you."

"She... No..."

Greg seemed lost for words. His piggy little eyes darted this way and that.

"She's a cow," he said at last, recovering some of his self-confidence. "A right cow."

Seb was indignant. Where did Greg get off calling Tara a cow? He managed to control himself. "In what way?"

"She just is. I don't have to give a reason. Least of all to you two losers."

"Greg asked her out," said Benny Gorman, sniggering. "She said no."

All the other gang members turned and stared daggers at Benny.

"What?" Benny said. "Greg tried to get a date with Tara and she said she'd rather go to the cinema with a serial killer."

"Benny," Greg growled. "Shut. Your. Stupid. Fat. Face."

Benny stopped sniggering.

"I'm sorry, Greg," he said. "It just slipped out." He looked so panic-stricken, it was almost pathetic. "You know me. Benny Bigmouth. Ha ha. Just can't help myself."

"When was this?" Seb asked.

"What's it to you, geek?" Greg shot back.

Seb kept his expression blank. "It's relevant to a matter we're involved with."

"Fortnight ago," Benny blurted out helpfully. "Last Friday but one."

"Benny!" said Greg, exasperated.

Benny Bigmouth hung his head. "Sor-ree."

"Well, there's your answer," Greg said to Seb. "Last Friday but one. Are we all done with the Guantanamo water-boarding?"

Seb glanced up at Frankie. "I think we've learned all we need to. Don't you, Frankie?"

"Because you can tell Tara from me," Greg said, "she's not getting a second chance."

"Huh?"

"That's why you're here, isn't it? You're like, what, playing matchmaker or something. Right? Tara's realised she made a mistake turning down my offer, and she's thought better of it and she wants me to ask her out again, only she's too shy to say so herself."

"Er, yeah," said Frankie uncertainly. "Something like that."

"Well, you tell her Greg says no way. Never in a million years. You get one shot with me. You don't grab it, that's your loss. Plenty more girls out there who'd kill for a date with Greg

Stubbs." Greg thumped his chest. "Tara missed the boat."

"Riiight," said Seb. "OK. We'll tell her that."

"Be sure you do." Greg whirled round. "Now then, Benny..."

* * *

Seb couldn't help but chuckle, when he and Frankie were far enough away.

"Tara and Greg in a tree, K-I-S-S-I-N-G," he chanted.

"Yeah, talk about unlikely."

"She's so out of his league. So far out, he can't even *see* her league from where he is."

"Try telling Greg that. Delusional!"

"Still, you can't blame him for trying," said Seb.

"Suppose not," said Frankie. "If skinny blondes are your thing, then you could do a lot worse than Tara. And that must give Greg a motive, don't you reckon?"

"I do. Only problem is, it doesn't really seem Greg's style. He's a thug, no question, but he's in-your-face. Texting threats? Just seems a bit wimpy for him."

"Yeah, but you saw how he acted. He's majorly embarrassed about the whole thing. He can barely bring himself to admit Tara knocked him back. Wouldn't that make him *more* likely to do something like send her those texts? No one would know he was doing it, so no one would see that she'd hurt his feelings."

Seb nodded slowly. "Yeah. Makes sense."

"So now we've got two suspects. Luke and Greg. We've just made our job twice as hard."

"And I have a feeling it's about to become *three* times as hard," said Seb.

They had just passed a poster advertising the production of *Grease*. There was a picture of a big 1950s American car with tailfins and a broad radiator grille. Next to it were boys in leather jackets and girls in pink satin jackets, all dancing.

Seb wheeled himself backwards and ran an eye down the cast list.

"There's one other person I'd like to have a chat with."

He pointed to the name of the girl playing Rizzo, leader of the girl gang in the musical.

"Millie Patel?" said Frankie, puzzled. "You don't think...?"

"Remember when the auditions were on?" said Seb. "And Millie was telling everybody she was a dead cert for Sandy?"

"But she didn't get the part. Tara did."

"And Millie went moping around for a week."

"Yeah, that's right," said Frankie. "She had a face on her like a slapped backside."

"She also got all her friends to stop talking to Tara. Tara used to hang out with Millie's crowd, then all of a sudden, no more sitting at the same table at lunchtime. Millie clearly hasn't forgiven Tara. Which all makes that text message – 'You don't deserve to be Sandy' – pretty relevant."

"Ahh. I see."

"Come on." Seb grasped the hand rims. "They're rehearsing right now. To the theatre!"

CHAPTER 8

HOPELESSLY DEVOTED

When they arrived at the theatre, Tara was running through her big solo ballad, "Hopelessly Devoted To You". She swayed to and fro across the stage, belting out the tune. Mrs Clements, head of music, accompanied her on a keyboard. Mr O'Hare kept shouting out instructions and encouragement from in front of the stage.

"That's it, Tara love. Keep your head up. Superb. Little bit louder here. This is Sandy baring her soul to the audience. She's crazy about Danny but he doesn't even care. Her heart is breaking. Yes!"

He even joined in at one point.

"'But... now... there's nowhere to hide since you pushed my love asi-i-ide!'"

Seb winced. "Ooh, my ears! Tara, on the other hand..." He gestured towards the stage. "Class act."

Frankie had to acknowledge that the girl had a great voice. She looked the part, too. The wide-eyed, all-American sweetheart.

Several other members of the cast were sitting in the auditorium, watching Tara. The exception was Millie Patel. She sat hunched in her seat, staring intently at the screen of her phone. Tara might have been on another planet for all Millie cared.

Seb rolled himself to the front of the auditorium, where he could catch Tara's eye. He wasn't sure whether she saw him or not. At that moment, however, Tara lost her way in the song. Mrs Clements played on, but Tara had forgotten the next line. Her voice cracked and faltered as she tried, and failed, to find her place again. Mrs Clements's accompaniment tinkled to a halt.

"Tara?" said Mr O'Hare. "Why have you stopped? Is there a problem?"

Tara stared around the stage in panic like a startled rabbit. Then, with a sob of dismay, she dashed off into the wings, covering her face with her hands.

"Tara!" Seb called out.

Mr O'Hare leapt up onto the stage and raced after her.

Seb wanted to follow her too, but he couldn't. There was no direct access to the stage from the auditorium for a wheelchair user. He would have to go back out the front entrance, round the corner of the building and in through the side door. He spun round and began making his way up the aisle.

"Whoa," said Frankie. "Where are you off to in such a hurry?"

"To catch up with Tara."

"Er, why?"

"You saw her," Seb said. "She just lost it up there, in front of all these people. It must be the pressure she's under. I need to go and comfort her. I can tell her about the progress we're making. It might make her feel better."

"Seb." Frankie looked stern. "You're one of the kindest-hearted people I know. But, as your friend and as your partner in crime-solving, I've got to say this to you. You're letting your feelings about Tara get in the way of the job."

"What?" Seb blustered. "I'm not – "

"You want to be her knight in shining armour,"

Frankie said. "That's fine. I get it. But Mr O'Hare's dealing with her. Millie is sitting right over there and we're here to interview her."

"But Tara – "

"Let Slaphead handle it," Frankie insisted. "Millie looks like she's sending a text – maybe another hate text to Tara. This could be when we catch her red-handed. Come on."

Seb hesitated. But Frankie was right. The way to help Tara right now was carry on hunting the cyber-bully.

"All right," he sighed.

CHAPTER 9

SUSPECT THREE: PRINCESS

"Millie?"

Millie looked round. "Yeah? 'Sup?"

"Can you spare me and Frankie a moment of your time?"

"No." Millie returned her attention to her phone. "Busy."

"Doing what?"

"Doing something called 'none of your business'."

"Sending a text, by any chance?"

Millie gave an aggravated grunt. "So what?"

"To Tara?"

Now Millie rolled her eyes. "And why would I be sending a text to Miss Gorgeous Knickers? To congratulate her on being so goshdarn *wunnerful?*" Millie said the last two words in a silly version of an American accent.

"Well?" challenged Frankie. "*Was* that what you were doing?"

"If you must know, I'm updating my Facebook status."

"Can I see?" said Seb.

Millie leaned across and shoved the phone under his nose. There was her Facebook wall. She was halfway through typing in her status. It read:

@ rehearsal. Bored out of my skull.
Drama teacher's promised me a go at
"There Are Worse Things I Could Do" but
I don't know if I'm going to get a chance
now because he's too busy

"Too busy doing what?" Seb asked.

Millie snatched her phone back. "Can't remember, now that you've butted in."

"Too busy fussing over Tara Adamski?" said Frankie. "Was that going to be it?"

"Probably." Millie's eyes narrowed. "This is a bit sus, you two being so interested in what I'm up to. Don't tell me, you're on a case."

"Yes," said Seb.

"And I'm involved?"

"You're a 'person of interest'." Seb had picked up the jargon from the many cop shows he watched. He was pleased to be able to use it in real life.

"Seriously? No kidding?" Millie seemed both irritated and delighted at once. "And what heinous crime am I supposed to have committed? Burglary? Blackmail? Murder?"

Her snarky tone didn't bother Seb and Frankie. They'd faced up to Luke Waterlow and the whole of Greg Stubbs's gang. A bit of needling from the likes of Millie Patel was nothing.

"You don't like Tara much, do you?" Frankie said.

"Oh no, I *adore* her!" Millie clasped her hands together and fluttered her lavishly long eyelashes. "She's simply divine. Why, she's my BFF of all BFFs."

"All right, we get the picture," said Seb. "She's not your favourite person in the world."

"Why wouldn't Tara be my favourite – after she stole Sandy from me?" Millie's voice curdled. "Mr O'Hare promised I was going to be Sandy, but then Tara waltzes into the auditions, all simpering and... and *American* – and bang, just like that, Slaphead forgets about me. *Drops* me. Suddenly he's all, 'Oh Tara, you sing so brilliantly, like an angel!' Girl couldn't carry a tune in a bucket."

Seb was about to protest on Tara's behalf, but Frankie leapt in before he could speak. "Mr O'Hare didn't 'drop' you, Millie. He gave you Rizzo. I've seen *Grease*." It was one of Frankie's mum's favourite movies. Leanne Keane would get out the DVD once a month on average, and she and her daughter would sit on the sofa and watch it together, munching popcorn and Toblerone. "Rizzo's way cooler than Sandy. She gets all the good lines, *and* a solo."

"But she's not the lead, is she?" Millie said. "What you may not realise, Frankie, not being theatrical, is that lead is everything. I don't think you'll ever tread the boards. You don't have the looks for it. Or the grace." Millie cast an eye up and down Frankie. "If you were an actress, you'd understand that your name has to be top of the bill. You don't want the best lines, you want the *most* lines. You want to be onstage longer than anyone else. That's how you make it in showbusiness. Second place is no place."

"So you resent Tara," Seb said. "You envy her."

"I wouldn't say that. She's got no talent, so what's to envy?"

"Her looks?"

"Hello?" Millie circled a finger at her own face. "Winner of last year's Miss Charrington junior beauty pageant. Runner-up in *Asian Girl* magazine's Search For A Pre-Teen Star competition. Looks? Not a problem."

"No," said Frankie. "Personality, on the other hand…"

"Ahem," said Seb. To Millie he said, "So you ditched Tara from your group of friends."

Millie shrugged. "She was made to feel unwelcome, that's all. And if it's all right with you, I've had enough of this. It's my life, my business. You can butt out."

"But – "

Millie dismissed them with a talk-to-the-hand gesture and an airy "whatever". She resumed tapping away on her phone.

Knowing they weren't going to get any more out of Millie, Seb and Frankie ambled off.

"So?" Frankie said.

"You want me to say she's the one, don't you?"

"I'd love that. Dragging Millie Patel in front of Mrs Broomfield, with proof that she sent the texts – it would make my day. Just to see the look on her prissy little face."

"Well, she could be," Seb said.

"But you're not sure."

"Her spelling on her Facebook status was perfect. Proper punctuation and everything."

"She could be faking it on the texts," Frankie said. "Making the spelling deliberately bad. And dissing somebody from a distance, by phone, that's definitely Millie's style."

They came out into the open air. Almost immediately, they heard running footsteps.

It was Tara, hair flying. She looked frantic and fretful.

"Guys! Guys! Thank God I found you. Look."

On her phone there was a new message. It had arrived just a minute earlier.

```
u got those 2 snoopers chasing
after me, well call them off, or
else
```

"Frankie and I don't snoop," Seb said, insulted. "We detect."

"He's on to you," said Tara, "and he doesn't like it. Maybe you should stop. Otherwise he might take it to the next level."

56

"I think it means he's rattled," said Frankie. "He knows we're closing in on him, so he's getting desperate. Or, should I say, she."

"She?" said Tara. "So you know who it is already?"

"We've narrowed it down to three likely candidates."

"Who?"

"Luke Waterlow, Greg Stubbs and Millie Patel."

Tara looked startled, but soon recovered her composure. "Makes sense, I guess. Luke – there was that cheating thing, of course. Millie's been awful to me since the casting for the musical. And Greg... Well, I'm kind of surprised. But he doesn't need much reason to be nasty, does he?"

"But," Seb added, "it may not be that straightforward. We're close to a solution anyway, Tara. Give us another day or so, and we should have this all worked out."

"You'd better," Tara said. "My pop's really on the warpath. I don't know how much longer it'll be before he lets the lawyers loose. And when he does – watch out everyone!"

She walked off, slipping the black phone into her blazer pocket.

CHAPTER 10

TRENDING

The following day, the school was ablaze with rumours. Word had got around that Tara Adamski was a victim of bullying. Not just that, but the bully had done something truly horrible to her. Nobody knew exactly what, but everybody had their own idea. Some said she had been beaten up. Others said she had had glue poured in her hair. There was even talk of a knife being used to threaten her.

It didn't matter that there was no evidence for these stories, or that Tara looked as good as ever. The rumours were exciting. People listened to them and passed them on, often exaggerating them in the process. It was a trending topic among Twitter users at the school, under the hashtag

#whohatestara?. Tara Adamski had become the eye of a storm of whispers and half-truths.

Somehow it became generally believed that Luke, Greg and Millie were to blame for the bullying. Seb had no idea how their names had leaked out. He hadn't told anyone else, and neither had Frankie. But, as Frankie pointed out, it wasn't as if she and Seb were working in secret. They had approached the three suspects openly; Millie might easily have talked about the investigation to on her social network; and with Benny Bigmouth in his gang, Greg had trouble keeping a lid on secrets.

People were soon giving Luke and Millie hateful looks. Greg likewise, although the looks that came his way were never nice at the best of times. Throughout the day an atmosphere built up around the three. Greg became more sullen and resentful than ever, and Luke and Millie seemed bewildered and alarmed.

Tara, meanwhile, was getting plenty of sympathy and attention. She took it well, with the air of someone who was being as brave as they could.

Soon another rumour started circulating. This one was about Tara's father threatening to sue

the school. Maybe Tara had leaked it herself. It only added to the feverish mood.

Seb drew Frankie aside after their art lesson.

"This can't go on," he said. "There are innocent people getting the evil-eye treatment. We've got to wrap this case up soon as possible."

"Agreed, but unless you know who the bully is..."

"As a matter of fact, I think I do."

"Well?"

"I can't say yet. But if we're going to expose who it is, we've got to do it properly."

"You have a plan?" said Frankie.

"Naturally," said Seb. "It'll take a bit of organising. Also, it's going to call on your petty larceny skills."

Frankie's eyes lit up. "Seriously? Where? When? I'm your girl." Frankie had a way with locks. They seemed to fall open in her hands. She joked that it was her *Britain's Got Talent* talent. Not that she would ever dream of using it except in a good cause.

Seb told her what he needed from her. "I, meanwhile, am going to write three notes and slip them into our suspects' lockers," he said. "And then we'll see what happens."

CHAPTER 11

CLOSING IN

The next day, after school, Tara, Seb and Frankie waited in an empty classroom.

"Are they coming?" Tara asked, for the umpteenth time.

"They'll come," Seb said. He wished he felt as certain as he sounded.

Finally, footsteps echoed in the corridor outside. It was Millie Patel.

"Here I am," Millie said. "Responding to your mysterious invitation. I wasn't going to bother, but then I thought why not?"

"I appreciate it, Millie," Seb said.

"So this is going to tidy up this whole mess and clear my name like your note said? People have been treating me really weirdly this past couple of days. Mostly that's your fault, though that scheming little witch Tara Adamski's got a lot to answer for. Oh, hi, Tara," she added brightly. "Didn't see you there."

"Hi, Millie."

The two girls exchanged frosty fake smiles. Millie sat down at a desk, as far from Tara as possible.

"Who else is coming?" she asked.

"Wait and see," said Seb. "Shouldn't be long."

Please hurry up, he thought. *Please don't let me down.*

Eventually Greg Stubbs and Luke Waterlow trudged in together. They looked surly, as usual, but also curious.

"Well, well, well," said Greg. "What are we here for?"

"To get at the truth," said Frankie. "Just like Seb promised."

"Truth about what?" said Luke. He gestured at Tara. "Her copying off me?"

"Sit down and you'll find out," said Seb.

"I just don't want to get sued," said Luke as he sat down. "Everyone's saying her dad's talking to lawyers about all this." He looked disconsolate. "I'm too young to be arrested."

"Ah, it's not such a big deal," said Greg, the voice of experience. He leaned against the wall, folding his arms across his beefy chest.

Seb drew a deep breath. "Right then," he said. "As you all know, someone has been sending Tara some pretty vile text messages this past couple of weeks."

"Yawn, yawn," said Greg, fanning a hand in front of his mouth. "Get on with it. Haven't got all day."

"Detention to go to, Greg?" said Frankie.

"As a matter of fact, yes."

"And I've got rehearsal in a minute," said Millie. "Let's hurry this up."

"Then I'll cut to the chase," said Seb. "If you could all three get out your phones."

"Why?" said Luke.

"Because there's one guaranteed way to smoke out the guilty party, and this is it. Come on. Your phones."

None of the three suspects moved.

"If you're innocent," Seb said, "you have nothing to worry about."

Millie shrugged. "Fair point." She produced her phone. Frankie took it off her and activated it.

"Greg? Luke?" said Seb.

Luke looked at Greg for guidance. Greg, with a great show of reluctance, handed his phone over to Frankie. Luke followed suit.

Frankie laid all three phones in a row on the desk in front of Seb.

"And Tara," Seb said. "Can I have yours too? Your black one."

Tara gave him the phone, with a frown of puzzlement.

"It's very simple," he said. "I'm going to call the number the texts have been coming from. Whoever's phone rings, that's who's been sending them."

"Oh," said Tara. "I get it."

"Then we'll know for sure which person in the room is the cyber-bully."

"Ah. Right. But you know..."

"What, Tara? Is there a problem?"

Tara shook her head. "No. It's just... If it's one of these guys, what's to stop them attacking me right here and now? Maybe this isn't such a good idea."

"I'm here," Frankie said, standing at Tara's side. "They'll have to go through me to get to you."

"Oh. OK. Thanks." Tara tried to look reassured.

"Here we go," said Seb. He pulled up the cyber-bully's number on the black phone. He placed his thumb above the screen, ready to hit the Call icon.

Millie threw a glance at her phone.

Greg eyed the ceiling.

Luke gnawed a fingernail.

"Ready?" said Seb to Tara.

She gave an anxious nod. She was shaking like a leaf.

"OK."

Seb touched the icon.

The three phones lay side by side, silent.

"Connecting," said Seb, studying the black phone's display screen.

Still silent.

Then a phone started to emit its ringtone. The sound was muffled, as though coming from someone's pocket.

The three phones on the desk remained silent.

The ringtone was coming from another corner of the room altogether.

Tara looked shocked. "Where is it? Whose phone is that?" She turned to Frankie beside her. "It's yours, isn't it?"

Frankie reached into her pocket and fished out a small, budget-range silver Nokia. She held it up so that everyone could see it. The ringtone was trilling out from its speaker, loud and clear.

CHAPTER 12

WHO DID IT?

"You, Frankie?" said Millie, aghast. "*You're* the one who's been bullying her?"

"Nice one," said Greg. "Go round blaming everyone else, when all along it's been you. I like that."

"I don't understand," said Luke.

"That's all right," said Seb. "I don't expect you to."

"This isn't my phone," said Frankie. "*This* is my phone." She dug out a different phone from another pocket and waggled it in the air before putting it away again. The silver Nokia was still ringing in her other hand. "This one doesn't belong to me at all. It's Tara's." She hit Disconnect, silencing it.

"You what?" said Greg.

"It isn't mine," Tara protested. "I've never seen that phone before in my life." There was a tiny tremor in her voice as she spoke. "I would never have one as crummy as that. Look at that one over there. Those are Swarovski crystals on it. That's the kind of cellphone Tara Adamski owns."

"That other phone *is* yours, though, Tara," said Seb. "You know how I know that? Because Frankie found it in your locker."

Tara gaped. "You broke into my locker?"

"Yep," said Frankie. "Wasn't hard. You use a combination padlock, Tara. With one of those, all you have to do is pull on the shackle while turning the number wheels one after another, from the base upwards. Each wheel gives a tiny little click when the correct number comes round. You can feel the wheel sort of settle into place, as long as you keep pulling on the shackle. Piece of cake."

"You're lying," Tara blustered. "Go through my things? You wouldn't dare."

"Then how come I know that your code is one-zero-two-nine?"

Tara looked flabbergasted.

"Which happens to be your birthday," said Seb. "I checked on Facebook. Twenty-ninth of October. You Americans write that as ten twenty-nine."

"Okay, so you broke into my locker," Tara said. "Well, that's a major breach of the school rules. You guys are going to be up to your necks in doo-doo."

"Are we?" said Seb. "Maybe. But it doesn't change the fact that we found that phone there And it's all in the memory, all the outgoing texts to your other phone, the black one here. The phone from your locker is a pay-as-you-go cheapie. It's the second one you've used for the job. You ditched the first after blocking the number, to make the whole thing look more authentic. No one's been cyber-bullying you, Tara. You've been doing it to yourself."

"But why would I do that?" Tara's voice rose, taking on a shrill, somewhat desperate tone.

"Yeah," said Luke. "Why would anyone do something so stupid?"

"Stupid?" Greg scoffed. "Totally flipping pointless, more like."

"I'll tell you why," said Millie. "To get us in trouble."

"Correct," said Seb. "All of you did something to upset Tara. Luke, you accused her of cheating."

"I think she did cheat."

"So do I. I think Tara isn't as good at chemistry as she wants us and her dad to believe. She copied those test answers off you. But then she thought you spotted her doing it, so she made it look as if *you* were the cheat. Isn't that right, Tara?"

Tara's face flared red. She fixed Seb with an evil glare. "So the chemistry-genius gene has skipped a generation. So what?"

"Meanwhile you, Millie," Seb said, "got all your mates to turn on Tara after you lost out on the role of Sandy. Not very mature, but still."

Millie looked sniffy but said nothing.

"And as for you, Greg..." said Seb. "Tara didn't take you up on your generous offer of a date. You've been bad-mouthing her ever since."

"And why not?" said Greg. "Only right and proper."

"In your head, maybe," said Frankie.

"Tara didn't plant a clue in her text messages that pointed to you," Seb continued. "Her main targets were Luke and Millie. When you turned up as well, it was a bonus. She seemed surprised when we told her your name, but not displeased."

"You know what?" Tara said. Her face was scrunched up like a ball of paper. She didn't look in the least bit pretty any more. "All right. It was me. I set the whole thing up, and I'm proud of that. I hate you all, you bunch of creeps! I'm Tara Adamski. My father earns more than all of your fathers put together. Poppa could send me to a private school, but he thought it would be good for me to get to know the *real* British people. Huh! Well, that was a dumb idea, wasn't it?"

She snatched her black, crystal-spangled phone off the desk.

"And you," she snarled, jabbing a perfect painted fingernail at Seb. "You're the worst of the bunch. You aren't nearly as smart as everyone makes out. Remember how I hugged you like that? Bawled my eyes out in front of you those times? I faked it, and you didn't even suspect. Making you think I admired you so much. 'Oh, Seb. Only you can help me. You're my only hope.' Well, newsflash. I was using you and your pal Frankenstein to get these bozos in trouble and show everyone you don't mess with me. And it almost worked too!"

"Tara," said Frankie, her voice as soft and cold as snow. "I don't mind you calling me

Frankenstein. I'll let that pass. But no one – *no one* – abuses Seb's trust and gets to brag about it."

"What're you gonna do, Frankenstein?" Tara taunted her. "Hit me? You lay one finger on me, and after Poppa's big-shot lawyers are done with you, your folks won't have a penny left."

"My mum doesn't have a penny anyway," Frankie said. "And no, I won't hit you, Tara. But the whole school is going to know about this stunt you've pulled. We'll make sure of that, won't we?"

She looked at Luke, Millie and Greg. They nodded in unison.

"And once we do, once the truth gets out, imagine what life here is going to be like for you. If I were you, I'd convince 'Poppa' you *have* to go to a private school. Because from this day on, your name's going to be mud at Charrington Secondary."

Tara recoiled, as though Frankie actually had punched her. She looked at all the angry faces around her. It dawned on her that she had just ensured that no one at this school would like her or trust her again, ever.

With a screech of dismay, she fled.

CHAPTER 13

ANSWERS

"So," said Luke, "how did you know Poor Little Rich Girl was bullying herself?"

"One clue was the spelling," Seb said. "Tara was trying too hard to make the texts sound as though they were coming from someone British. You know how Americans spell some words differently from us? Like 'labour'. We put a 'u' in it, they don't. But when it's part of the word 'laboratory', there's no 'u'. Tara put one in. She didn't realise the spelling of 'laboratory' is the same in both languages."

Luke didn't follow Seb's explanation. He said, "Ohhh," all the same, as if he did.

"Also, there was that thing about teeth," Seb went on. "It seemed more like something an

American would *think* a Brit might say. We're not as obsessed with dentistry as Americans seem to be."

"So you knew all along it was Tara?" said Millie, frowning.

"Not at first, no. I had a feeling she wasn't being totally straight with us. But it wasn't until she gave that little performance on the stage that everything began to fall into place."

"Her song?"

"The way she broke down halfway through. She was doing fine up till then, warbling away, not a care in the world. Then she must have spotted me in the auditorium and remembered she was supposed to be living in terror. Cue sudden panic attack." Seb tutted at himself. "I should have clicked sooner than that, though. Tara... She confused me."

"By being so super-friendly," said Frankie.

"Exactly." Seb glanced down, embarrassed. "I was an idiot."

"No, you weren't," said his friend. "Tara used her looks to take advantage of you. But you saw through it in the end."

Greg shoved himself away from the wall and retrieved his phone from the desk.

"I'm off," he said. "I'll get extra detention if I'm late for this one. But for what it's worth... Keane? We're quits now. But I want you to teach me that trick with padlocks."

"Not sure that would be wise," said Frankie, "but maybe."

"And Ford?" Greg's expression turned strange. He looked as though he was trying to smile, or trying not to. "You done me a favour today. Won't forget it."

He left the room, with Luke in tow. Millie followed them out. She was already on her phone, logging on to her Twitter account to start tweeting about everything that had happened.

"Greg Stubbs just congratulated you," Frankie said, wide-eyed. "Wonders will never cease."

"Yeah, right. Makes up for everything," Seb said with a hollow laugh.

"Seb. Listen. I'm sorry about Tara. Some girls are just like that. They manipulate boys, because they can."

"Some boys do the same to girls," Seb said. "Just for a moment, though, I felt that it was possible."

"What was possible?"

"That someone like me could have a chance with someone like her."

"What do you mean, 'someone like you'?"

"A geek. Uncool. A brainiac." Seb slapped the armrests of his wheelchair. "Stuck in one of these things."

Frankie bent over him. "Listen to me, Seb Ford. Tara – any of the Taras of this world – would be lucky to hang out with you."

"You reckon?"

Frankie rolled her eyes. "And he's supposed to be the smart one on the team! Now come on." She grabbed the wheelchair's push handles. "Let's go celebrate. Ford and Keane crack yet another case. Off to the newsagents. The mint Magnums are on me."

"Do I have a choice in the matter?"

"Nope."

Seb smiled. "You big bully."